EVERY WITCH WAY

Demon Hunter

Every Witch Way

Jason M. Burns

Darby Creek
Minneapolis

Darby Creek
An imprint of Lerner Publishing Group, Inc.
241 First Avenue North
Minneapolis, MN 55401 USA

For reading levels and more information, look up this title at www.lernerbooks.com.

Image credits: zef art/Shutterstock (zombies); hxdbzxy/Shutterstock (clouds); Rosen Graphic/Shutterstock (texture); idwan kurnia/Shutterstock (font); PERFECT_VECTORS/Shutterstock (font).

Main body text set in Janson Text LT Std.
Typeface provided by Adobe Systems.

Library of Congress Cataloging-in-Publication Data

Names: Burns, Jason M., 1978–author
Title: Every witch way / Jason M. Burns.
Description: Minneapolis : Darby Creek, 2026. | Series: Demon hunter | Audience term: Teenagers | Audience: Ages 11–18 | Audience: Grades 7–9 | Summary: After a classmate summons a powerful demon, it falls on Damon and his friends to fend off a swarm of zombies and send El Presidente back where he belongs.
Identifiers: LCCN 2025012263 (print) | LCCN 2025012264 (ebook) | ISBN 9798765670637 library binding | ISBN 9798348028169 paperback | ISBN 9798765691823 epub
Subjects: CYAC: Demons—Fiction | Zombies—Fiction | Ability—Fiction | Friendship—Fiction | High schools—Fiction | Schools—Fiction | Salem (Mass.)—Fiction | LCGFT: Paranormal fiction | Novels
Classification: LCC PZ7.1.B88535 Ev 2026 (print) | LCC PZ7.1.B88535 (ebook) | DDC [Fic]—dc23/eng/20250320

LC record available at https://lccn.loc.gov/2025012263
LC ebook record available at https://lccn.loc.gov/2025012264

Manufactured in the United States of America
1 – TR – 12/15/25

To Hunter and Eloise—hunt down what makes you happy in life and don't be afraid to face your demons.

1

There he is. Walking along the sidewalks of Essex Street as if he doesn't have a single care in the world. Which, he probably doesn't. But given the fact that I'm tracking him, he should. To me, he's the enemy. But to everyone else going about their day, he's just another random visitor capable of helping the local economy.

Tourists. Salem is filled with them, especially when everyone wants to dip their toe into the spooky pool come Halloween. Even now, with spring having just sprung, there is still a steady flow of unfamiliar faces with unfamiliar auras wandering the cobblestone streets and historic cemeteries. It's weird being from a place known for its horrific past. It's even weirder watching people come from all over to celebrate that past.

For those unfamiliar with my hometown of

Salem, Massachusetts, this is where the Salem Witch Trials went down back in 1692. Dozens of people were accused of witchcraft. It was a real abracadabra panic. In the end, nineteen of the accused were hanged and one more was pressed to death for good measure. (You don't want to know the details of that one other than it, you know, involved pressing.)

Now, people come from every nook and cranny of the world to take a picture in front of the old tree that served as the gallows. Usually, they're wearing a kitschy T-shirt that reads, "I *Hung* Out Under the Murder Tree."

Stay classy, Salem sightseers.

But here's the thing. While I can't say with any certainty if any of those accused of witchcraft during the 17th century were *actual* witches, I can say with absolute certainty that this is a place that draws in evil. How do I know that? Because I can see demons, and let me tell you, there's a lot of them around here.

Take this guy that I'm tracking, for example. Even though he looks like a middle-aged man with a receding hairline, I know better. That is a shadow demon perusing a rack of clothing at the shop across from the café where I'm currently conducting my stakeout. He doesn't know that I'm watching him. Unless you can see the world the way I do, there are no telltale signs that he is anything but human.

For as long as I can remember, I've been able to see auras. What's an aura, you ask? Think of it as a personal fingerprint for a soul—a living energy that surrounds the body. Until I was about seven and mentioned it to my mom in passing, I thought everyone could see them. I had no reason to believe otherwise. It was my mom who actually showed me what a special gift being able to see auras was. She was also the one who taught me how to *read* an aura.

Believe me, when it comes to auras, seeing and reading are two very different things.

If you stepped up to my table where I'm sitting right now sipping from my Persian-style iced tea, I could tell you more about yourself than you could tell me. By reading your aura

I'd know if you're creative, kind, empathetic, anxious, courageous, or even asthmatic. You could be all of those things . . . or none of them.

Some people are more likely to show off the traits that I try to avoid in people. Callous, controlling, cruel, and compulsive—the four Cs of the self-absorbed. Those are the kinds of people whose auras suggest they're capable of causing bad in the world. But as it turns out, bad can't hold a gift shop witch candle to evil.

I lift my drink to my mouth, only I don't take a sip. This is a signal. One of my best friends, Madelyn, is seated on a bench across the street about ten feet from our villain of the week. She holds an umbrella over her head even though there isn't a cloud in the sky.

Madelyn was born with albinism. Her skin is so fair that the sun can give her a serious burn in only minutes. Umbrellas, hats, long-sleeved shirts, and sunscreen are her allies. Accepting my signal, she reaches into her hooded sweatshirt and pulls out the controls for Screech, our team's airborne support system, which she named after her favorite breed of owl.

A demon's aura looks dramatically different than a human's. Madelyn's, for example, is colorful and shimmery. It looks like mica, a kind of rock Mom and I used to collect on our hikes throughout the White Mountains of New Hampshire. I could stare at it for hours.

The demon across the street has an aura that is nothing like Madelyn's. It's devoid of color altogether and instead looks like the chaotic, tantrum-inspired scribbling of a toddler. If I were to stare at it for more than five minutes, I'd get a headache.

Not all demon auras are like this, but most of them present as a warning sign to people like me who can see beyond the everyday and into the extraordinary.

"Damon, what do you know?" Liam's voice asks from over the walkie-talkie I have tucked away in my backpack. He's my best friend who also happens to be a trickster demon. Sure, that fact made things a little complicated at first. But we worked it out. Liam's strength is his, well, strength. I've seen him bench-press a trailer full of cows.

I reach into the bag and press down on the talk button. "A lot. Like, for example, did you know that the scientific name for the American buffalo is actually *Bison bison bison*?"

Liam doesn't respond.

"The genus is bison, the species is bison, and even the subspecies is bison. Wild *and* redundant, right?"

Liam still doesn't respond. I've alienated myself again.

"Sorry," I explain. "Boo-en read a book on the history of Yellowstone National Park to me last night."

Liam's voice finally returns. He sounds annoyed. "I meant, what have you learned about the demon we're tracking."

I look up from my backpack just in time to watch the subject of our investigation steal an "I *Hung* Out Under the Murder Tree" T-shirt.

"That he has incredibly bad taste, *and* he's on the move," I inform Liam, trying to create as little of a scene as possible while talking to my backpack. I watch as the shoplifting demon turns away from the storefront and heads off down Essex Street, tripping on every other cobblestone just like all the tourists who visit the downtown area. "He's moving in the direction of Charter Street."

"Word," Liam confirms. "I'll meet you at the cemetery. We'll bring the baddie down there."

I chug the last of my beverage. "Roger. I'll have Madelyn send in the drone. Don't approach until I'm there."

But by the time I'm out of my seat and dumping my cup into the recycling bin, Liam's walkie is already offline. He's gone rogue. Again.

Leave it to a trickster to automatically defer to trickery.

2

The rule of thumb when going up against a shadow demon is that you never face one alone. Unless the light source you're standing in is positioned directly above you (and thereby causing you to cast no shadow at all), the demon can—and will—hide in your shadow.

As I round the corner of Essex Street and look directly into the Friends Burial Ground, I see Liam learning this lesson firsthand. He is spinning around in circles trying to grab hold of the demon as it dips in and out of his shadow. The demon jabs at Liam, punching him over and over as Liam clearly can't step away from his own shadow.

"You should have waited for me before you tried to bring it down on your own," I say as I push open the creaky cemetery gate. I sound way too much like my dad for my own liking.

The shadow demon reaches out from its hiding spot inside Liam's shadow and slaps my friend across his face. Now that I'm closer to the action, I can tell that the demon has shed its fake human skin. It looks like a blob of spilled ink in the shape of a hairless mountain goat.

"Would you save the 'I told you so' stuff until *after* you help me!" Liam barks as he rolls underneath the slashing claws of the demon.

I reach into my backpack and pull out a pocket-sized mirror that once belonged to my mom. I hold it out in front of myself and aim the reflective surface directly at Liam's shadow. A lot of demons hate to look at themselves in their true form.

I'm hoping this trick works on shadow demons.

The demon lunges out from Liam's shadow and wraps its long, spindly fingers around my neck.

As I try to suck air into my lungs, I quickly realize that mirrors definitely don't work on shadow demons.

"How you see I?" the demon asks. For most demons, English is not their first language. Some don't speak it at all.

I don't answer. Not because it's a secret. I don't answer because I can't. The demon's hands are squeezing my throat too tightly. I'm unable to speak at all.

Thankfully, I wasn't the only backup.

Screech descends down from the canopy of newly-sprouted oak leaves above us as the demon continues to choke me. I redirect my eyes to Madelyn, standing in the shadow of an above-ground mausoleum. She's busy working Screech's controls. I hope I make it clear with my pained expression that I don't have much air left in me.

Even with no visible eyes, the shadow demon turns to look up at the drone. "That what is?"

Screech hovers overhead. Madelyn fiddles with one of the knobs on the controls and the drone dips its nose downward. The shadow demon now looks up at a thin hose that protrudes out from the front of Screech.

"*That* is bath time," Madelyn yells out as she jabs her thumb into a red button on the controls.

A stream of holy water erupts from the drone. Ours is a special blend. We have it blessed and prayed over by a representative of every conceivable religious movement in the county, no matter how small. It's potent stuff. And I'm happy to say, demons hate it.

Screech douses the shadow demon in the holy water, causing it to howl and hiss. It releases its grip on my neck and recoils. I take a deep breath. The air fills my lungs. I felt close to passing out there for a second, and I'm relieved to still be standing upright.

"Keep it coming!" Liam hollers out to Madelyn, doing his best to sidestep any splatter.

As a demon himself, Liam would have a similar reaction if any of the water were to hit him directly.

Madelyn continues to shower the demon while I reach into my backpack and pull out a neatly-folded shroud. For those who don't know, a shroud is a piece of fabric used to wrap someone in after they die. Much like our holy water, this particular shroud is special.

Said to be thousands of years old, the swatch of yellowed cloth is embroidered with ancient symbols. None of us, not even Liam, can read them. Honestly, we have no idea what they say, but we do know that the shroud is effective at anchoring demons in place.

"Do it!" Liam shouts as the demon peels away from its shadow. The creature is now exposed. It's dancing a pained jig on the grave of some long-departed soul as it tries to shake off the holy water that's singeing.

I unfold the shroud with a snap of my wrists. It catches in the breeze coming off the nearby Atlantic Ocean and waves like a flag. The shadow demon snarls as I drape the magical fabric over its head. The demon instantly goes stiff, freezing where it stands.

"I thought we agreed to be more careful this time," Madelyn says as she shuts down the stream of holy water coming out of Screech's nozzle.

"Don't look at me," I say, pulling a jagged hunk of bright green malachite from my pocket. "It was Liam who wanted to be a one-man action star."

Liam sighs, kicking the immobilized shadow demon in its exposed shins. "That's for stowing away in my shadow." Liam turns to look at me. "And frankly, I'm sick of always playing by your rules, Damon. Your way isn't the only way things get done, FYI."

"I never said it was," I tell Liam as I fiddle with the malachite. "I just don't want any of us to get hurt."

Liam doesn't respond. He knows I'm right. If he didn't, he'd never shut up about it. If speaking your mind were an Olympic sport, Liam would be the most decorated gold medalist of all time.

I raise the malachite to my mouth. The relatively rare copper carbonate mineral is the only known way to openly communicate between The Pit, the place where the demons are from, and the human world. This particular chunk originated in Russia and is essentially a direct line of contact to my demonic insider Boo-en. He is a paralysis demon who prefers human interaction over hanging out with other demons.

"Okay, Boo," I say into the rock. "Everything is in place. You're up next."

The brilliant green malachite glows. This signifies that Boo-en has received my message.

Within moments, there's a flash of auburn light beneath the shadow demon's feet. The light is a portal—one of Boo-en's, which expands outward in all directions until it's big enough to swallow the shadow demon whole. The demon slips down, dropping into the void in our reality and falling out of sight. Boo-en's portal, meanwhile, shrinks to a pinhole and disappears, too. The shroud floats down to the ground.

"Well, it doesn't matter how it started," I say, slipping the malachite back into my pocket. "In the end, the hunt was still a success."

"Whatever," Liam snorts, pushing past me as he marches toward the cemetery's entrance. "I'm out of here."

I bend down and pick up the shroud, shaking it off before folding it back up. "Are you seriously running off to pout?"

"You wish," Liam says, pushing through the gate with such force that it rips one of its hinges from the rock wall it's attached to. "I have homework to do."

Madelyn steps up next to me. We both watch as Liam storms off down Charter Street before taking a sharp right turn on Essex and disappearing out of sight.

"What's been going on with you two lately?" Madelyn asks.

I shrug. "Not sure. We just haven't been seeing eye to eye the last few days. Maybe he's mad at me for something."

Madelyn spins around to look at me. "Have you asked him?"

I actually haven't. I'll let him cool down a bit and then I'll text him. I'm sure everything will be back to normal by the morning.

3

I tried to text Liam last night. He never responded. This morning he wasn't on the bus. I'm not sure if it was an accident or if he purposely missed it to avoid me. Either way, he made it to school today. I saw him running down the hallway just after I got to my locker.

I must have done something to tick him off. I just don't know what.

"How could you do that to me?!" a girl's voice shouts loudly somewhere behind me.

I finish stuffing my books into my locker and then turn around to see what the commotion is all about. Bella, a quiet sophomore who has fallen head over heels for Salem's Gothic charms, is standing in the middle of the corridor with tears streaming down her face. Her dark mascara melts away from her lashes, dirtying her pale face. These aren't tears of sadness, however. These are tears of anger.

"What's wrong, can't think of a good enough excuse yet?" Bella continues shouting as a group of curious onlookers—myself included—gathers.

I realize that Bella is yelling at Addie, her best friend. I have numerous classes with both of them. Although extremely different in their personalities and interests, Bella and Addie seem inseparable.

I guess I'm not the only one having BFF problems.

"Quiet down, Bella," Addie whispers. "You're making a scene."

Asking her to quiet down only makes Bella scream louder. "What's wrong? Afraid your little 'goth accessory' is going to embarrass you in front of your teammates?!"

Addie is good at basketball. Like, *really* good. She has single-handedly put the Salem Broomsticks on the map. She is already a local sports legend at sixteen and one of the top college recruits in the country. Her game is legit.

"Please," Addie pleads, taking note of all the curious faces now staring at her, "can we just talk about this in private?"

Bella lets out a fabricated laugh. It's meant to inform Addie just how ridiculous her suggestion is.

"You'd like that," Bella responds. "Talking about your friends in 'private' has become one of your favorite pastimes. I can only imagine all of the other things you've said about me to people. I'm sure they are all *super* positive."

That last part is dripping with sarcasm. It doesn't take a psychologist to analyze what has happened between these two. I don't know the full details, but I know it involves one of them—Addie—speaking out of turn.

I wonder if Liam is mad at me for the same thing?

Between the screaming and the crowd that has gathered, it is only a matter of time before one of the faculty members comes along to see what the commotion is all about. Miss Torres, the new physics teacher, is apparently the responsible adult to draw that short straw because she pushes her way through the blockage of students clogging up the hallway.

"What is the meaning of all of this?" Miss Torres asks no one in particular. Looking at her complicated aura full of entangled colors makes my eyes hurt. "I'm quite certain all of you have a third-period class to get to."

Before turning away from Addie and letting the thickness in the air dissolve, Bella scowls one last time. "Good luck at your game tonight."

Although it wasn't said with any particularly evil emphasis, it's clear that Addie takes the parting shot as a threat. "What is that supposed to mean?"

No answer comes, however. Bella walks off to class as Miss Torres shoos off the rest of the students.

As the kids head off in different directions, I spot Liam standing on the other side of the hallway. He's staring at me. Scratch that. He's *glaring* at me. It's the same look Bella was just giving Addie.

I reach out, ready to say something, but Liam dismisses my attempt at conversation and walks away.

I wasn't overthinking things. He really is mad at me.

Fractured friendships. Apparently, they're all the rage.

4

Madelyn, Liam, and I like to keep things mobile when it comes to our meetings.

We tend to gather and discuss rumors of demonic activity in places where kids our age would normally hang out without raising any unnecessary red flags. You know, like an occult bookstore. It was my dad who first discovered the three of us meeting at Coven Hardcovers. He thought it was weird that we were there, so we stopped going. Now we have meetings in parks and at fast-food restaurants.

Today we are in our gymnasium sitting high up on the bleachers "cheering on" the Salem Broomsticks. Addie and her teammates are set to take on their rivals from the local prep school, the East Salem Salamanders. By all accounts, it should be a very lopsided match up in favor of the home team. Last time they played the private school squad, Addie broke the single-game scoring record.

As for Madelyn, Liam, and myself, our squad is one teammate short.

"Liam's not coming," I say to Madelyn as she shifts herself on the wooden bleachers next to me. The bleachers are impossibly uncomfortable. "The way he looked at me this morning, you would have thought I sent him through Boo-en's portal instead of that shadow doughnut."

When we're in a public place talking business, we always refer to demons as *doughnuts.* Why we think that the word *portal* is appropriate for a high school basketball game, though, is still not crystal clear to me.

Madelyn turns to look at me. "I told you. Talk to him."

"I tried!" I exclaim, my voice squeaking louder than the sneakers on the court below. "I texted him multiple times. I even tried to call him. On the phone."

On the court below us, the volunteer referee—gym teacher Sid Santori, a man who never met a pair of jeans he didn't prefer turning into shorts—blows the whistle. It's the official start of the game. The ball rockets upwards from his hand. Addie and her Salamander counterpart launch up after it. The jump ball ends with Addie empty-handed and looking quite confused.

"If we are going to get back to tracking down doughnuts, we need you two to fix whatever is broken between you," Madelyn says while redirecting her attention to the game. The Salamanders score on their first possession and then quickly get the ball back as they steal it away from Addie.

I rub my face in frustration, trying to wipe away my frown. "I know. And I want to. I just don't know what else to do."

Back down on the court, Addie tries to block one of the Salamanders from scoring an easy layup. Mr. Santori blows his whistle and calls her out for a foul. Goaltending.

Madelyn pats my knee. "Don't worry. It will figure itself out. The three of us are too good of a team to let anything mess up our mission. Or our friendship."

Do you know who else is too good to be messing up this much? Addie. But she just lost control of the basketball again. Her attempted pass soars into the bleachers where it lands like a rock. Visibly frustrated with herself, Addie jogs over to the Broomsticks bench as a Salamanders fan tosses the ball down to Mr. Santori.

"Weird," I say, watching Addie as she speaks with her coach along the sidelines. "I've never seen her so unfocused in a game before."

"It must be going around," Madelyn responds. I know that her comment is meant to put my own mind back on track. After all, we're here to talk business, not actually watch the basketball game.

"Right," I acknowledge as I turn back toward her. "So, what have you heard? Any new flavor of doughnuts popping up in town?"

Madelyn digs into her backpack and pulls out a spiral notebook. She opens it to a bookmarked page and consults a paragraph of scribbled notes.

Seriously, her handwriting is almost as bad as Addie's game play today.

"Nothing solid. However, there were some rumblings of a horned creature spotted on a couple's doorbell camera three nights ago. We may want to check that out."

I hear Madelyn speak, listing off the doughnuts, but she's right . . . I'm distracted. I don't absorb anything that she's telling me because I'm too focused on trying to figure out what I could have done or said to make Liam upset with me.

"Oh," Madelyn continues, "also, someone anonymously DM'd our socials to say they heard the new motorcycle gang seen riding around town was up to no good. That one seemed outside of our supernatural jurisdiction. I forwarded the message over to Salem PD." Madelyn turns to the next page in her notebook, which is empty. "And that's all she wrote. She being me, of course."

Down on the court, Addie finds an open lane and dribbles the ball toward the Salamanders' net. This is a shot she has made with ease one hundred times before. But as she lifts herself into the air to take the shot, her feet get tangled up. The basketball erupts awkwardly from her hands, springing upward and clanging off the underside of the rim. She falls to the floor in a defeated heap, cursing herself as she does.

What is going on with everyone today?

5

Dad offered to pick me up after the game, but I told him that I'd rather walk home. It was barely dark when I left school. The spring air is cool and saturated with the scent of fresh lilac. It is a much better option for my senses than his clammy patrol car that reeks like pork rinds.

Also, walking gives me time to think. Liam is my real-deal best friend. And we've defied the odds to get there. He, a mischievous trickster demon. Me, a demon hunter.

I met him in middle school. I knew what he was as soon as I set eyes on him. But back then, I wasn't busy hunting demons. I just played a lot of video games, and it turns out, so did Liam. We hit it off, first in a virtual world, and then in the real one.

The fact that we could find common

ground at all is, frankly, astonishing.

He's astonishing.

And I miss him.

I'm mindlessly kicking a rock along the sidewalk when I sense someone coming up behind me. They're not making enough noise to be riding on a scooter or a skateboard, but they're definitely moving too quickly to be casually walking in my direction. They're on a mission, and that mission is me.

I take one step forward, plant my front foot, and then pivot myself around in one fluid motion to face the opposite direction. My hands are clenched in fists, and I'm prepared to use them. Being a demon hunter, I had to come to terms with the fact that sometimes the tables turn and I'm the one being hunted. I have to know how to defend myself.

But those skills will not be necessary today.

"Sorry if I scared you," Addie says as she peeks out at me. She's tucked behind a telephone pole so that only the top half of her body is visible.

I let my fingers rest. The fists are now

more like paddles.

"Addie? Are you following me?"

She steps out from behind the telephone pole. She's still wearing her game jersey. She dances nervously back and forth, her feet fidgeting almost as much as her hands.

"Not really," she says. "I was actually trying to catch up to you."

"Oh," I say, not really understanding things any clearer. "Well, consider me caught."

Addie and I have always been friendly, but I wouldn't call us friends. The last time we spent any substantial time together outside of school was in kindergarten. My mom had arranged a playdate for us. I spent the afternoon over at Addie's house.

I don't remember much about it other than her mother making us lunch. Grilled cheese sandwiches. Except, unlike the ones I was used to, Addie's mom used provolone cheese. I didn't even know that grilled cheese sandwiches could be made without American cheese. It seemed so fancy, like I was experiencing high society.

"Can we talk a minute?" Addie asks.

"What about?"

Addie pulls me off to the side, pressing both of our shoulders up against a fence that lines the property running along the street. Even though we're alone—at least as far as my eyes can tell—she whispers everything else that comes out of her mouth.

"I've heard . . . rumors about you, Damon."

I shrug, scraping my shoulder along the fence. "Welcome to high school, right?"

She shakes her head emphatically. Much like my dad after his favorite football team loses a game, Addie appears agitated.

"No. No. No. Not those kinds of rumors, Damon. Not kid stuff. People talk, you know. They say things. They say you . . . communicate with monsters."

Even though it's cool, verging on chilly, I'm suddenly sweating. "Monsters? That's odd."

Addie keeps speaking. "Not just any monsters." She pauses and looks around, making sure we're still alone. "Demons."

I back away from Addie, slipping into the darkness of a nearby shadow. I don't want her to see how nervous I am. "Addie, I'm not sure who you're hearing those kinds of things from, but . . . they're ridiculous. I'm the son of a single dad—a cop. He believes in a world that is black and white. Good and bad. That's the world I grew up in. We don't believe in demons."

Addie steps forward, extinguishing the empty space between us. She grabs hold of me and shakes me like a rag doll. "I'm cursed, Damon. Cursed! I found information online about a demon who can remove curses if you summon him and make the right offerings. If I don't summon him, I'll never be able to play basketball again." Her eyes go wide like a pair of floodlights. "I saw you at the game. You were watching. You saw how badly I was playing. I couldn't even control the ball."

"You're not cursed," I tell her. "Whatever you're stressing out about, you can talk to someone about it. An adult. They can help you."

"No!" she screams, no longer worried about who may be wandering by. "I won't be able to get the college scholarship my mom and dad are expecting of me if I do nothing. Please, help me summon the demon. I can't disappoint my parents."

Now it's my turn to step forward, which I do with authority. I get as close to Addie as I can without actually touching her. Instead, I focus on the seriousness of my icy-cold tone.

"Stop, Addie! Whatever you think is going on . . . it's not that. Under no circumstances should you try to summon this demon. You don't know what kind of power you're playing around with."

I peel away from her and turn to head home. Whether she stands there and stares at me until I disappear out of sight, I don't know for sure. I refuse to look back. She needs to know how serious I am, whether that reveals my secret demon-hunter identity or not.

6

I've been working on my biology homework for over an hour, and I've gotten as far as . . . my name. That's it. My name on a piece of paper. Not exactly an efficient use of my dwindling time this evening.

I'm just having so much difficulty focusing. I keep racking my brain, trying to figure out what I could have done to make Liam so mad at me. We went from two peas in a pod to the pod splitting wide open and both of us rolling away from each other. And it seemed to have happened in record time, too. It just makes no sense.

There is a knock at my bedroom door. It's a welcome distraction.

"Come in," I say, leaning back in my desk chair.

My dad, dressed in his Salem police

uniform, pushes the door open and steps inside. His freshly polished badge catches the overhead light and bounces it back into my eyes, forcing me to lean my chair even farther back. Out of instinct, he motions for me to lower my headphones before realizing that I don't have any on.

"What up?" I ask.

"I'm headed out for my shift," he says, waving his thumb toward the surface of my desk. "How's the homework going?"

I feel myself losing control of my leaning chair and sense that I'm only seconds away from falling backward. I quickly correct myself and readjust the chair so that it is in the full upright position.

"It's going," I respond to my dad after regaining my equilibrium.

My dad leans over and takes in my empty sheet of homework paper. "You sure about that?"

I sigh even though I don't mean to. "It's fine, Dad. I'm just getting a slow start. It will get finished."

He lets it go.

"I left some dinner in the microwave for you," he says, adjusting the gig line of his pants.

Gig line is an old military term that references the perfect line a soldier needs to maintain between the buttons of their uniform shirt, belt buckle, and pants zipper. I only know this because a few weeks ago Boo-en read *The Complete History of Naval Terminology* to me while I was sleeping. Remind me to tell you all about the *muster station* after I finish my homework.

"It's your favorite, saag paneer."

"Thanks, Dad," I say, returning my attention to my blank sheet of homework paper.

My dad nods. "Well, I'm on an overnight, but I should be back before you hit the bus for school. Remember to keep the front door locked, the dowel in the slider, and to call me on my cell if you have any problems."

Eyes. Still. On. Homework.

"I will."

"And don't lean back in your chair," he

adds. "You're going to fall."

Once a cop, always a cop.

My dad backs out of my bedroom and eases the door shut. I run my hands over my head and give myself a quick pep talk.

I have to focus. This homework isn't going to write itself.

Before I can heed my own advice, I feel the hair on the back of my neck rise and wriggle. A familiar surge of energy circulates through my bedroom. There is an almost inaudible *pop, pop, POP* of electricity at my back, which I only recognize because I know what to listen for.

I glance over at my alarm clock. "It's too early," I say to myself.

I get up and look out the window. My dad is backing his patrol car out of the driveway. To be safe, I run to my bedroom door and lock it just as a portal between this reality and another appears above my bed.

Boo-en appears from out of the portal and flops down onto my mattress, mimicking a classic cannonball dive as he does. The floor shakes as his gangly body bounces off my bed and then flies back up into the air where he remains, floating silently.

Boo-en is a paralysis demon. He looks like a cross between a prehistoric weasel and a modern-day llama, but with the ability to walk semi-upright like a primate plucked from one of the lowest rungs on the evolutionary ladder. He is hideous to look at, and his aura isn't much better.

Paralysis demons feed off of humans as they sleep. The "food" they're searching for is physical energy—the stuff that gives you that get-up-and-go attitude in the morning. If you wake up each day feeling like a slug, chances are good that you're being visited by a paralysis demon and you don't even realize it.

Boo-en was shocked to discover that I wasn't scared of him when I woke up in the middle of his first feeding session one night. In fact, we struck up a conversation as he sat on my chest and siphoned off my energy. By the time he was full, we were fast friends.

Now we have what we like to call a gentleman's agreement. I allow him to pop into my room every night so that he can feed, and he promises to read from the nonfiction books I leave out.

I'd heard that the unconscious brain can absorb knowledge even while you sleep. So now, I get to have all these random facts at my disposal that I would otherwise not have time to learn. I just have to make sure that I drink a protein shake before I go to bed so that I can balance out what I'm putting into my body and what Boo-en is taking out.

"What the heck are you doing here so early?" I ask him, pointing to the clock for backup. "You know I don't usually go to bed for at least two more hours."

"Boo-en is not here to eat and read," he says, hovering above my bed. "Boo-en is here to tell you of big goings-on in the demon realm."

One of the other benefits of being friends with someone like Boo-en is that he is a great source of information. Sure, he's a demon, but he prefers the company of humans to his own kind, which means he isn't afraid to sell any one of them down the river.

"How big are we talking?" I ask.

Boo-en floats down to the bed and sits on the edge. His long, spindly legs hang off the side, waving back and forth like a sickening metronome.

"Damon's world is in big trouble," he responds. "A scary demon crossed over. Not a lesser demon like Boo-en. This demon is powerful. It is the president of The Pit."

I raise an eyebrow. "The Pit has a president? Did you vote?"

Boo-en launches himself off the bed and grabs me by my shoulders. I can see the fear in his red, pupil-less eyes. "Damon is not taking Boo-en seriously. This demon will destroy Damon's world. This demon can command legions of other demons. This demon will bring *total* destruction."

"How did it cross over?" I ask, finally understanding the seriousness of the situation.

Boo-en's aura surges with a dramatic shift in color. It goes from a sort of granite countertop camouflage to a raging inferno of bright oranges and reds. To date, his aura is the only one I have ever witnessed that can change its overall pattern and color. This goes for demons or humans. It seems to coincide with whatever emotion he has bubbling up to the surface.

"El Presidente was summoned by a human."

I swallow so hard that I half expect to choke on my tongue. "By any chance, what powers does this demon have, Boo?"

The aura that surrounds Boo-en pulses with a deeper, warmer yellow. It's like looking at a distant landscape of transforming trees in the fall. "El Presidente has so many powers. Boo-en already said this."

"I know," I tell him, still hoping for some sort of further clarification. "But what would a human summon this demon for?"

"Boo-en cannot say for sure. Boo-en can only speculate. Maybe . . . to remove a terrible curse? Boo-en thinks this a bad idea, though. It is more terrible to be indebted to a demon, especially one like this."

I gasp, which causes Boo-en to flinch.

She actually did it. Addie summoned a demon. I have to get over there right away.

7

I hop on my bike and head off in the direction of Addie's house. I have every conceivable item I know of that can hurt a demon stuffed into my backpack. According to Boo-en, none of them will do me any good against this "president" of the underworld. In fact, Boo-en tends to think this demon is pretty much indestructible if the summoning spell was properly performed.

The good news just keeps on coming.

I should have done more to convince Addie that summoning demons—*any* demon—was bad with a capital B. I should have explained what I know and how I know it. That would have helped Addie understand that opening a door for some super powerful being to pass through would not end well for anybody. I just hope I'm not too late to fix it.

I pedal my bike as fast as my legs will allow. I know where Addie lives. It's only about three blocks from Madelyn's house. I texted Madelyn and Liam before I left and told them to meet me over there. Madelyn responded instantly and said she would leave right away. Liam didn't respond at all. We could really use his trickster strength on this one. I'm praying he shows up.

As I get closer to Addie's neighborhood, I notice a red-orange glow hovering over the houses in the distance. It reminds me a lot of Boo-en's agitated aura. Then I smell smoke. Thick, choking smoke. The kind that comes from the burning of more than just wood.

I steer my bike along a winding, downhill S-curve as it cruises into Addie's neighborhood, passing the Citrus Acres sign on my way. I cross over three connecting streets and then make a right turn on the fourth, Clementine Way. I'm too late. Addie's house is engulfed in flames.

I see two silhouettes standing off to the side. They are completely backlit by the raging fire, but I still recognize them. Madelyn *and* Liam. My prayers have been answered.

I skid to a stop in front of my friends and leap off my bike. I don't even bother using the kickstand. Instead, I just let the bike fall to its side and clang onto the concrete.

"Where is Addie? Is she safe? Did she—" I hesitate.

Both Madelyn and Liam stay focused on the burning house. They are mesmerized by the flames. In the distance, I can hear the unmistakable sound of sirens headed in our direction. I worry that Dad will be one of the first responders and that I'll have to explain why I left the house without letting him know.

"We haven't seen her," Madelyn says. "We haven't seen anybody."

Liam doesn't respond. He doesn't even acknowledge my arrival. I want to confront him and put whatever this is behind us, but I know it's not the time or the place.

Before I can ask a follow-up question, I hear whimpering coming from Addie's backyard. It's not a dog or a cat or any other animal. It's a human's whine.

With Madelyn and Liam following me, I rush into the backyard. Addie is kneeling about thirty yards away from her fire-consumed house. She's crying. I sprint to her side.

"Thank goodness you're okay," I say, checking her over for burns or other injuries. "You are okay, right?"

"I did this," she confesses in a catatonic monotone. "I did."

"What about your parents?" Liam asks. "Are they safe?"

Addie nods. "Not home. They are at a work dinner. I was alone. In . . . there. It's why I thought I could . . ." She trails off. "I did this."

I notice that the sirens no longer sound like they're getting closer. They're still wailing, but it's like they've been frozen in place somewhere on the way to Addie's house. This demon isn't powerful enough to freeze parts of reality, is it?

"Addie, I need you to tell me what happened," I say to her. "Did you go through with the summoning spell? Is there a demon here?"

Addie turns away from the burning house and looks directly into my eyes. "I just wanted to be able to play basketball again. I didn't know it would do all of this."

I feel my heart skip a beat. "What is *it*, Addie?"

"It came up out of my bedroom floor like my carpet was some kind of puddle of putrid water," she answers, her eyes filling with tears. "It just rose up and smiled at me, and then my floor went back to normal."

"It's going to be okay," I tell her, trying my best to comfort her.

"Is it?" I hear Liam ask sarcastically as he points toward the house. "Because *that* makes me think *not so much*."

8

I look up from Addie and follow Liam's finger to the back of the burning house.

There, stepping out of the flames, is what appears to be a man wearing a bright yellow suit. He—though really, more of an it—casually walks through the fire, though neither it nor its snazzy ensemble are burned by the flames.

As it gets closer to us and emerges from the inferno, I can see that its eyes are the same color as its suit and that it has a single horn—like a rhinoceros—sticking out of its forehead. The horn is at least three feet long and curls upward as it gets closer and closer to the terrifyingly pointy tip.

I squint my eyes, focusing on the demon's aura. It looks like a bowl of rotten fruit, moldy and bad for your health. This has to be

El Presidente.

The demon steps out onto the back porch of the house and grabs hold of the railing. It leans forward and begins to stretch its quads like a runner readying for a race. Upon seeing the demon, Addie's tears turn into panic. She begins to hyperventilate.

El Presidente glances down from the porch and takes notice of us. But it doesn't seem at all concerned by us being there.

"Well, look at you four little *poops*," it says, just as surprised as we are by the childish insult that spits from its mouth.

The demon's black tongue flickers out of its jaws like a snake as it switches positions, stretching out its other quad. It seems as relaxed as an outsider from another plane of existence could ever hope to be.

"That was weird," it continues without being prompted by any of us. "I could have sworn I said *poops*." It pauses and tries again. "*Poops*."

I fling off the backpack from over my shoulders and unzip it. Instead of digging around to find the right working tool for the job, I simply hold the bag open and then slide everything inside toward the demon. El Presidente looks down at the pile of random religious symbols and iconography and smiles.

"Is that smattering of doohickeys supposed to worry me?" the demon asks, slowly descending the stairs of the back porch. It pauses as it reaches the backyard, and then it kneels down and picks up an ancient Irish cross I purchased in an online auction a few months back. It has helped us banish a half dozen demons since it arrived by mail. Tonight, not so much.

El Presidente brings the cross to its mouth and bites down on it. With its sharpened teeth, it tears off a chunk of the artifact and chews it like an overcooked piece of steak—eventually turning it into sawdust, which it quickly swallows. The demon then discards what remains of the cross over its shoulder, tossing it into the fire.

"This is, frankly, quite pathetic," it says, pointing to the lot of us. "Four children? This is who opposes me?"

Liam steps forward, hands clenched in fists. "I'm no child. I'm a demon. Just like you. And I'm about to kick the *poop* out of you."

Moving with the speed of a bullet train, the creature is suddenly in front of Liam and has its hand wrapped around my best friend's neck.

"My boy, *no one* is like me!"

With the flick of its wrist, El Presidente throws Liam into the surrounding forest. Liam is as durable as a steel pole, so I know he'll be safe when he lands, but the fact that this creature could so easily toss him aside has me more than a little bit concerned.

The demon looks away from us and sniffs at the air like a bloodhound. "Let me save you the headache. You don't stand a chance. The last time I was summoned to this horrible little hovel of an existence, the entire Roman army—complete with a sea of well-trained legionnaires—was called to dispose of me. Naturally, I kicked all of their *bottoms*."

Once again, the word that comes out of the demon's mouth is not the word it had intended to say.

"Can I not swear here?" it asks, though none of us are prepared to answer. "Ah, fiddlesticks. It's no matter. It's the thought that counts, am I right?"

As I try to push my shock aside and come up with a game plan, the demon completely loses interest in us. It looks around, taking in the human world.

"We can't let you leave," I say, though I know deep down that I can't make it stay either.

El Presidente turns its eyes to me—each of which looks like a blazing sun—and offers up what I believe to be a sympathetic smile. "Aw. That's so cute."

It reaches out and flicks me in the forehead with its middle finger, which in turn sends me flying backward at least thirty feet. Thankfully, I land in the somewhat soft embrace of a hydrangea bush. My ears ring like the bell of a department store Santa looking for a donation.

"Now if you'll excuse me," the demon says,

"El Presidente has some *heck* to raise."

And with a snap of its fingers, El Presidente disappears in a plume of bright yellow smoke.

9

I don't realize that I have passed out until I eventually wake up again.

In the back of an ambulance.

"Easy," Madelyn says to me, pushing me back down on the gurney as I try to sit up. "That demon scrambled your head pretty good when it sent you airborne. I'm worried you may have a concussion."

I take in my surroundings, trying to make sense of the time that is now unaccounted for due to my unconsciousness. I see Madelyn and Addie sitting in the back of the ambulance with me. Liam is nowhere to be seen. I hear the sirens overhead, churning out their warning screams. I feel the scratchy sheets rubbing uncomfortably against my skin. I smell rubbing alcohol and disinfectant.

What I'm unable to locate are any of the

actual paramedics who should be tending to my injuries.

I reach up and paw at my head. My fingers track over a bandage that is wrapped around me like a last-minute mummy costume.

"I hope it's not too tight," Addie says optimistically. "I only took one CPR class and I'll be honest . . . I wasn't really paying much attention."

Now that she mentions it, the bandage is a little tight. Can the top of a head lose circulation?

"I don't understand. Why would you be the one to wrap my head up? Why wouldn't the paramedics do it?"

Liam's voice booms to life somewhere behind me. "Because they're all completely frozen like the rest of the adults in Salem."

I shift myself on the gurney and turn to the side so that I can look over my shoulder. Liam is driving the ambulance.

"What are you doing?!" I shout, white-knuckling the side of the gurney out of self-preservation. I know for a fact that my best friend does not have a driver's license.

"Relax," he says while adjusting the rearview mirror so that he can look back at me. "I'm like 127 years old in human years. Plenty old enough to drive a car."

I kick my feet off the gurney and sit up. "This isn't a car. It's a—presumably—stolen ambulance."

Madelyn leans forward and checks my bandage. She loosens it, quickly relieving my "am I going to get a numb brain" stress. As far as friends go, she's the prefect combination of sternly hardened and naturally nurturing. I've seen her scare the color right out of a demon, but I've also seen her nurse a sick bird back to health. She's so awesome.

"Liam is telling the truth," Madelyn says. "As far as we can tell, El Presidente has put a pause on everyone over seventeen. There are no adults to help. It all hinges on us tonight."

I rub my head. I try to gauge the severity of my injury and decipher if it's something I can easily hide from my dad when—no, *if*—this all gets resolved. Judging by the still-growing lump sticking out of my forehead where the demon flicked me, I'd say I'm going to have some explaining to do.

"Do we have any idea what this demon wants?"

No sooner do I ask the question than the ambulance slams into something with a dismissive thud. I feel the mystery item pass under the ambulance's tires, creating two speed bumps in quick succession that Liam doesn't slow down for.

"Please tell me that wasn't a body," I beg with about as much optimism as I can muster.

Liam takes one hand off the steering wheel and waves off my fearful inquiry. "Not a live one, anyway!"

Panicked by the implication of Liam's statement, I rise to my feet and turn toward the front of the ambulance so that I can see out through the windshield. All around us, ambling in all directions, are zombies. Yes, zombies!

Some of them are so beyond the point of decay that they're no more than walking skeletons with out-of-date clothing hanging off their bony frames. Liam drives the ambulance right through one that is wearing a loose linen shirt and dark pants. The entire zombie explodes into a plume of bone fragments and dust.

"Was that a Puritan we just drove through?" I ask.

Madelyn grabs hold of me and turns me around. She looks me right in the eyes. "So, here's the thing. The demon appears to be raising the dead all over town. It's hitting up each cemetery in a systematic approach. As far as we know, there's nothing at our disposal to stop this demon, so we're going to try a Hail Mary."

"Hail Mary?"

It's Addie's turn to speak now. The fear and disbelief that had gripped her earlier have subsided. "I suggested magic. My friend Bella—if I can still call her that—dabbles in witchcraft. It's why I stupidly summoned this demon in the first place. I upset Bella, big time, and she put a curse on me that made me unable to play basketball. I wanted the demon to remove the curse, but instead, it just laughed at me and then burned my house down. Maybe there's a spell that can send it back. That's assuming Bella will even help us after what I did to her."

Addie lowers her head. I can relate to how she feels.

"Heads up, gang!" Liam declares from the driver's seat. "We're here!"

Liam slams his foot down onto the brake pedal and jerks the steering wheel to the left. The ambulance fishtails. The rear comes forward and smashes into a pair of undead sightseers as it skids to a stop. Madelyn opens the back doors. I can smell the still-burning rubber of the ambulance's tires. Through the open doors we can now look out on Bella's house, which sits atop a sloping hill on the outskirts of town. Between us and her front porch is a roadblock of eager-looking zombies.

10

The zombies are still. They don't seem to want to attack us. Not yet. I assume they're waiting for us to get out of the vehicle.

"I'll run point," Liam says. He unbuckles his seat belt and climbs into the back of the ambulance with the rest of us. "I'll take as many of them down as I can while you three work your way up the hill to Bella."

Liam steps up to the opening at the rear of the ambulance. He cracks his knuckles, and a grin appears on his face. The zombies moan in excitement. It seems like each side is just waiting for the other to make the first move.

"What are you waiting for?" Addie asks.

The grin on Liam's face stretches even wider. "Dramatic effect."

Liam leaps out of the ambulance. His feet slam down onto the pavement. The sound causes the zombies to flinch a little. Without skipping a beat, Liam arches his back and looks up at the sky. He lets out a monstrous howl. He could easily be mistaken for a werewolf.

Recognizing the howl as a war cry, the zombies waste no time. They sprint—though, really, it's more of a fast-paced shuffle—toward Liam. As the rest of us climb down out of the ambulance, one zombie is already trying to wrap its arms around Liam. Liam rolls underneath the attack and then counters with an uppercut. I can't be sure if it's because of Liam's demon strength or his opponent's lack of muscle tissue, but the zombie's head flies off its rotting neck and soars through the air. It lands off to the side of the road, directly in front of a Salem PD patrol car.

"Oh no," Madelyn says, seeing it at the same time as I do.

Sitting in the front seat of the police car, frozen behind the wheel, is Officer Sheldon Dowling. My dad. The driver's side window is rolled halfway down, and he's holding a bag of pork rinds in his hand.

I take one step in the direction of the patrol car, but my path is quickly blocked by a zombie wearing a faded blue dress. If it had any lips, they would be snarling at me.

Someone, or something, grabs my shoulder from behind. I instinctively turn to defend myself. The grabber isn't a zombie, however. It's Addie.

"Don't worry about your dad," she tells me in a soft, gentle tone. "From what we can tell, the zombies don't want any part of the adults. It's us they want."

My face twitches. I'm not sure if it's because of the potential concussion or my sudden desire to cry. "I can't just leave him there," I plead.

"The best way for us to help him and the rest of the adults is to unfreeze them. And the only way we can do that is to clean up the mess that I made by summoning that demon in the first place. We need to get to Bella."

I hate to admit it, but she's right.

I back away from the patrol car as Liam charges in from outside my periphery and drives his shoulder into the zombie that was blocking my path. The putrid figure collapses into itself like a dying star. Its bones rattle on the pavement.

"Go!" Liam shouts. "Head for the house! Now!"

Madelyn, Addie, and I flee toward Bella's house. We chug up the steep hill. I'm tired halfway up, but I refuse to let the physical exertion slow me down. The zombies standing at the top of the hill have other plans, however.

"Grab hands and then spread out!" Madelyn orders. "We can use our arms to clothesline them!"

Like most of Madelyn's plans, this one straddles the line between genius and insanity. Also, like most of her plans, it totally works.

Madelyn grabs Addie's hand. Addie grabs my hand. Instead of stopping to face off with the zombies, we just run straight through them while we're all linked together. Our attached arms hit them at their necks, and they're thrown off their feet. I look back over my shoulder to see their various body parts and pieces rolling down the hill. At the bottom, Liam continues to pound the horde into dust.

"Uh-oh," Addie mumbles under her breath. Her heels skid to a stop, digging into the dirt. Madelyn and I are forced to stop along with her.

Standing in front of the stairs leading up to Bella's house is the biggest zombie I have ever seen. Even though this zombie has clearly gone through some pretty advanced stages of decomposition, there is still a lot of meat left on its bones. It is a hulking husk with an exposed rib cage. A nervous rat is hiding inside the darkness of its chest cavity.

"I don't think our clothesline trick is going to work on that thing," I say.

The zombified giant groans. *Mroooooorn.* It reaches into its own chest, wedging its hand between its ribs. A couple appear to crack from the pressure, but it doesn't seem to care. After a few seconds of digging around inside of itself, the hand returns holding the rat. The zombie smiles and bites down on it, snacking on the rodent.

I'm pretty sure that is an image that will haunt me for the rest of my life.

Before we can formulate a plan on how to get around the beast, a powerful gush of water hits the zombie in the side of the head. The distraction interrupts its snacking and causes pieces of flesh to peel away from its skull.

I turn my head and look at the source of the water. There is Bella, standing at the side of her house holding a garden hose. Her fingers firmly hold down a souped-up nozzle attached to the mouth of the hose.

"Hurry up and get inside!" she says as she continues to pelt the zombie with water. "I don't want to look at these things any longer than I have to!"

11

Bella's house is eerily quiet as Madelyn, Addie, and I slip in through the front door. Bella follows us in, dropping the garden hose on the welcome mat outside. She locks the door behind us, punctuating the action by collapsing against the door and exhaling deeply.

"Don't forget the deadbolt," I suggest, even though I don't like the sound of the word as it comes out of my mouth, given the circumstances. How about we call it an *alive*bolt instead?

Bella spins around and twists the knob of the *alive*bolt. The inner mechanisms turn, sending the steel bar—the bolt itself—into the door's frame. I can hear the lock click into place.

"Wait!" Addie says. "What about Liam?"

"He's fine," Madelyn answers. "As you now

know, he's not like us. Not exactly. He'll keep all the zombies away from the house so that we can plan our next steps."

Bella looks downright confused. "Not like *us*? *Who* is the *us*? Next steps? Would someone please tell me what is going on? Why are you here? Why are there zombies on my front lawn? Why are there zombies at all?" She steps away from the front door and points into the kitchen. "And why are my parents frozen in place like a couple of pieces of petrified wood?"

I move into the kitchen. The smell of a recently-served dinner—something with a marinara base if I had to guess—fills the air. Bella's dad is standing at the sink. His suspended body is stuck in the act of scrubbing a dish.

I step closer, walking around his right side so that I can see his face. His expression is calm, almost peaceful. I lean in, looking for any sign of movement. If there is any, it's too small for my eyes to decipher.

And that's when I spot Bella's mom. She's sitting at the kitchen table, which butts up against the doorway that I just entered through. She, too, is rooted in place, just like her husband. She's leaning over the table, which is covered in an incomplete jigsaw puzzle of birds of New England. She holds what appears to be the peak of a pileated woodpecker's red crest between her fingers. I lean forward and carefully pluck the piece away from her.

"What are you doing?" Madelyn whispers.

I shrug. "I couldn't help myself," I say quietly. "Boo-en read me the entire Audubon bird guide during winter break!"

I bend forward and push the piece into place.

"Seriously?" Bella says, annoyed by my prying fingers. "You came all the way here, through whatever *that* is outside, to help my frozen mom finish her birding puzzle?"

"We can explain," Addie tells her friend. She starts speaking so fast that I can barely keep up. "Or, I can explain. After all, this is all my fault. First I upset you—which is totally justified—and I totally hate myself for it. And then I tried to take the easy way out after you cursed me. I summoned a demon instead of just coming over here and apologizing. Now I've ruined everything, including our friendship. And apparently, the entire town."

Bella's confusion deepens. "Curse? What curse?"

Addie lowers her head in shame. "The one you put on me after yelling at me in the hallway earlier today."

"Addie, I didn't put a curse on you."

"Sure you did. And I deserved it, too. I said those things to my teammates about you because I was . . . insecure. I wanted them to like me. At least for more than my basketball skills." Addie begins to cry. "The last thing I wanted to do was to make you feel bad. I can't . . . I can't lose you."

There is an extended moment of silence. It fills the room, making the air heavy to breathe. Madelyn and I glance at each other.

The awkward silence lingers, and for a brief moment, I wonder if we've been frozen in place like the adults of Salem. Bella puts my fears at ease, however. Her feet slide across the tiles of the kitchen floor and stop in front of Addie.

"You haven't lost me," Bella tells Addie. "I was hurt, sure, but I would never cast a spell on you or anyone. You know that's not how I view magic. I believe it should be used for good. Only good."

Addie is easily a foot taller than Bella, so she has to look down to make eye contact with her. "But I was awful out on the court today. I couldn't sink a single shot. If you didn't put a curse on me, then why was I playing so poorly?"

As much as I want to help Bella's mom fill in the chestnut-sided warbler that is still missing a few pieces of its wings, I know my time is better spent trying to move this reconciliation along.

"You were never cursed," I say. "The truth is, those rumors about me are true. I can identify demons because I can see auras. A demon's aura is much different than ours. But so are the auras of the cursed. If you were cursed, I'd be able to tell by looking at your aura. It would be . . . tainted."

As she so often does, Madelyn brings her voice of reason into the conversation. "You're clearly upset about what happened between you and Bella. You're feeling guilty, too. I would bet that the stress of everything just threw you off your game today."

"That can't be right," Addie says, shaking her head. "I've never played so badly in my life."

"Well, you've probably never played without your best friend in your corner either," I tell her. "I speak from experience . . . that can really mess you up."

Addie is quiet. She breathes in and out. In through her nose. Out through her mouth. After circulating some fresh oxygen into her body, her posture goes slack. It's like the weight of the world has been lifted from her.

"I'm so sorry," Addie says, directing her apology at Bella. "For what I said. For trying to sweep it under the rug like it was no big deal. For assuming you'd try to hurt me. For everything. Can you ever forgive me?"

Now it's Bella's turn to breathe and relax. A tiny smile appears on her face. "Maybe if you could help me unfreeze my parents?"

Addie and Bella engulf each other in a bear hug.

Addie leans away from Bella. "Actually, we came here because we were kind of hoping you could help us."

Before Bella can respond, the relative silence of her home is shattered by the sound of breaking glass coming from the living room.

We rush out of the kitchen to find Liam lying on the living room carpet below the now broken picture window.

"That big fella out there sure is strong for a decomposing corpse," he says as he rises to his feet.

"Are you okay?" I ask, wondering if there is a reconciliation in our future as well.

Liam dusts the shards of glass off his shirt. "I'm fine. But we should probably get going. The demon we're after must have raised another cemetery because there's a second wave of zombies showing up."

Addie turns to Bella. "Can you grab your spell book? We'll fill you in when we're in the ambulance."

"Oh, about that," Liam says. "The zombies kind of . . . flipped it. We're going to need alternative transportation."

Bella's eyes go wide, and her eyebrows raise up into her forehead. "How would you feel about my mom's minivan?"

12

I'm wedged between Addie and Bella in the backseat of the minivan. Madelyn is in the passenger seat and, once again, Liam is behind the wheel. It's dark inside the van because we're still enclosed in the garage.

Madelyn reaches up and presses the button on the garage door opener, which hangs from the passenger seat visor. There is a shift in gears and the grinding of metal on metal, and then the door slowly begins to rise. We all turn around to see what kind of chaos the world has built up while we were tucked away safely inside Bella's house.

"There are hundreds of them," Addie says, her voice distant. It sounds like she's losing confidence in the mission.

Liam presses his foot down on the gas pedal. The engine revs.

"What they have on us in numbers, they lack in durability," he says, shifting the vehicle into reverse.

The minivan surges backward through the open garage door. The zombies all turn in our direction. The minivan plows into a small horde of them milling about in the driveway, knocking them away like bowling pins. *Striiiiiiiike!*

Liam jerks the steering wheel to the side and spins the minivan around as it reaches the road. He shifts it from reverse into drive and presses down on the gas pedal once again. I glance out at my fossilized father in his patrol car as we pass. A zombie stands nearby eating from Dad's bag of pork rinds. He's going to be so mad.

"Okay, so what am I supposed to be doing with this exactly?" Bella asks, patting the book of spells that sits on her lap.

Madelyn turns herself around in the passenger seat so that she can look back at us. "We need a spell that can help us send this demon back to where it came from. Our usual tricks and gadgets have no effect on it."

Liam drives through a long line of zombies, knocking them down like dominoes. *Click. Click. Click. Clack.*

"Um, you do know that I'm a sixteen-year-old who just *dabbles* in witchcraft, right?" Bella asks.

Addie reaches out over me and rests her hand on top of Bella's. "We know we're asking a lot, but we really need some help here. We're not asking you to open up the gates to the underworld, but maybe there's something in your book that we could use as a work-around?"

Bella offers up a timid smile and then nods. She opens her book and begins flipping through the pages. I glance down at them. They're yellowed and frayed, like a pair of old jeans, and filled with handwritten incantations that I can't make much sense of.

Liam turns his head slightly away from the road ahead, addressing the group as a whole. "Aside from anywhere other than back there, exactly where am I driving this rig to?"

Madelyn pulls her phone out of her pocket and activates the app that allows her to track what Screech is seeing. The drone is well above the streets of Salem, looking down on a familiar plot of old headstones.

"I've had Screech following the demon in stealth mode," she says, zooming in and out on the picture. "It looks like we're headed back to the Friends Burial Ground. The dead are about to be raised there next."

"Great!" I say sarcastically. "That's where a bunch of the accused witches were buried during the witch trials. That's just what we need—witch zombies!"

Bella becomes agitated as she flips through the pages of her book. "This is a lot of pressure. I'm not sure I'm the right girl for the job."

"You're the *only* girl for the job," I tell her. "Other than magical means, we have no idea how to take this demon down. It literally took a bite out of an ancient crucifix."

Bella swallows hard. Her nerves are getting the best of her. "Is that supposed to make me feel more confident? I mean, if you wanted me to reinvigorate a drooping dandelion or cut your chihuahua's nails without a working pair of available nail clippers . . . that I could do with this book. But I'm not some kind of level one hundred mage or . . ." She pauses mid-sentence.

"What is it?" I ask.

Bella turns in my direction but looks past me at Addie. "You had to recite a spell or incantation or perform a ceremony of some kind to summon this demon, right?"

Addie nods emphatically while saying, "Yeah."

"Hang on!" Liam shouts from the front seat. We all stiffen up as the minivan plows through a crowd of zombies. I see a pair of two-tone wingtip derby shoes flying midair as we continue through the cloud of raining zombie parts toward our destination.

"I did recently learn about a spell on one of the online witchcraft advice groups I regularly visit," Bella casually continues, as if we didn't just drive through a bunch of dead people. "It's called the Clip Hex. It quite literally clips five seconds from the past. No more. No less."

Liam glances up at us through the rearview mirror. "I don't see how five less seconds of this nightmare scenario is going to help us make it right again."

"I do!" I announce, leaning forward in excitement. "And it's genius."

"Go on," Madelyn says, urging Bella to share the details.

"Well, if Addie had to perform whatever she performed exactly right in order for the red carpet to roll out for this demon, we could essentially make it incomplete by chopping five seconds off of whatever she had to do or say. If the ceremony was not done correctly, the door would have not opened . . ."

"And none of this awfulness would have happened!" I finish.

"See," Addie says with a smile to Bella. "You're amazing. I knew you could do it."

"Thanks," Bella responds, "but it's not exactly a sure thing. For starters, you can't perform the Clip Hex without the hair of a demon, and it's not like we just have one of those ly—"

Madelyn reaches over and plucks a hair off Liam's head, causing him to shriek in pained surprise. The minivan swerves as we turn onto Essex Street, creating S-shaped skid marks on the pavement below.

"You were saying?" Madelyn asks as she reaches back and hands the strand of hair to Bella.

13

Bella sketches a symbol on the sidewalk outside of the Friends Burial Ground with a piece of purple chalk. Addie is crouched down next to her. She's holding open Bella's spell book so that Bella can copy the images that are drawn inside.

Madelyn has quietly snuck around to the other side of the cemetery. Her job is to lend aerial support with Screech should Liam and I need it.

As far as the plan goes, Liam and I are expected to go in there and keep the demon busy for as long as we can. Bella thinks she needs about fifteen minutes to complete the Clip Hex. Given how quickly the demon tore through Liam and me the last time we faced off, this promises to be the longest fifteen minutes of my life.

Liam and I stand at the gate of the cemetery. From our vantage point, I can just make out the silhouette of the demon creeping around inside. I know who it belongs to because I can recognize its horn as it passes behind the two-hundred-year-old grave markers.

"So, are we okay?" I ask Liam as we stall at the entrance.

Liam sighs. "Can we just go and do this before there are more zombies to deal with?"

I am completely unsatisfied with Liam's answer. I turn to him.

"No. That doesn't work for me. We're about to square up with the most dangerous demon we've ever faced. Odds are not in our favor that one or both of us comes out of this cemetery alive. I need to do this with a clear mind. I need to do this knowing that we are still . . . us."

There's an extended period of silence, something a place like this—a cemetery—is used to. I'm not. Very seldom do Liam and I not know what to say to each other.

"Listen," Liam eventually starts, pausing again before continuing. "I don't really know what you want me to say."

"What did I do?" I ask.

I hear monotonous moaning coming from inside the cemetery. It sounds like the dead aren't staying that way for long.

"Last Thursday," Liam says with a level of sadness to his voice that I've never heard from him before. "Do you remember what we did that day?"

My brain shuffles through some recent memories, trying to connect the dots between the present and the past.

Thursday was a curriculum day, so we had school off while the teachers did whatever they do during those at-home holidays. Madelyn, Liam, and I spent the day working a case.

A fast-food taco joint was constantly having its meat replaced with seasoned cardboard. Employees thought the restaurant was haunted, but after some investigating, we learned otherwise.

"The Mexican restaurant," I say. "We

found out the assistant manager was a demon, and we sent it back to where it belonged."

Liam laughs, but it's not the kind of laugh that implies he's having a good time. It's sarcastic, the kind of laugh that says there's *nothing* funny about what we're talking about.

"*Belonged* is an interesting word choice."

"What do you mean?" I ask Liam. "It was a demon. Sending them away is what we do."

Liam shakes his head, disappointed in my inability to read between the lines. "Never mind. You'll never understand. Let's just get this over with."

Liam steps through the gates of the cemetery, but I reach out and stop him from going any further.

"Wait! That doesn't resolve anything. We need to be able to put this behind us, Liam. If we are going to—"

"It was a trickster, Damon!" Liam shouts. "The demon you were so eager to cast off—the one you had such nasty stuff to say about even though all it did was switch out some ground beef for ground cardboard—it . . . was . . . a . . .

trickster! If it belonged somewhere else, where exactly do *I* belong?"

I stand there, stunned and ashamed. I have gotten so used to thinking about Liam as my best friend that I have failed to acknowledge him for who he actually is. I'm staring right at him, but he isn't feeling seen.

"Liam, I . . ."

A zombie appears in front of us at the entrance to the cemetery. Mostly skeleton, it has a single patch of flesh hanging off its skull. The patch is gray and dried out, like a piece of mummy meat that was glued to its face for fun. The zombie is covered in dirt. It has just climbed its way out of the ground and into my nightmares.

Liam squares up his shoulders with the zombie. He delivers a jab to its chin, knocking its jaw off. He follows the jab up with a hearty cross to its chest. The zombie crumbles into a heap.

"Come on," Liam says, kicking the fallen zombie parts aside. "It doesn't matter. Let's just get this over with."

"Why doesn't it matter?" I ask.

Liam walks into the cemetery, disappearing into the darkness. "It doesn't matter because I'm just another demon."

14

"Aren't you two scrappy little scabs a tenacious pair," El Presidente says as the demon spots us walking toward it.

El Presidente is currently standing over a grave. Between the darkness and the age of the tombstone, I can't make out who the resting spot belongs to. Before we can respond, El Presidente knocks on the ground with its fist and smiles at us. Within moments, a bony hand bursts out of the dirt and the unidentified dead is climbing its way to freedom.

"I hope you don't mind that I'm bringing some of these fine folks back for the party I have planned," the demon states. "My guest list is a mile long, which of course makes sense when you think about how many people have died since you climbed your way out of the primordial ooze."

Liam grits his teeth. "There isn't going to be a party because we're going to stop you from sending out the invitations."

El Presidente raises an eyebrow. "Are we still talking in metaphors, or do you literally think I'm throwing a party?"

Liam shifts his stance and then drives his foot forward, kicking the zombie aside. It smacks into a nearby tree and cracks in half, falling to the ground. The zombie's top half crawls toward us, dragging itself inch by inch with its hands. Its bottom half throws a toddler-like tantrum, pounding its legs up and down. The noise seems to wake the residents of the cemetery because more hands start popping up out of the soil.

Liam charges El Presidente. He wraps his arms around the demon's legs—a legitimate double-leg takedown, which I know about because Boo-en read me a book on collegiate wrestling not too long ago—and tries to muscle it to the ground. But El Presidente is too strong. I hurry in to help, wrapping my arms around El Presidente's torso. I manage to pin the demon's arms to its sides, but it does little good. Both Liam and I hold on for dear life as El Presidente bucks like a bull in a rodeo, sending our legs up into the air. I holler out into the darkness, hoping that Madelyn can hear me.

"Now would be a good time for a distraction!"

"Who are you *flogging* talking to?" the demon asks, growing more annoyed by our presence with each passing second.

Even with the moans of the undead permeating the cemetery, I can hear the low-flying hum of Screech descending from above. I feel something grab hold of my ankle. I turn around to see Prudence Danworth sticking up from out of her grave. We've never met, but I know who she is by reading her faded tombstone.

Prudence is trying to pull me down into her casket, which is a simple wooden box with as much rot attached to it as Prudence herself. I can smell the funk of the three-hundred-year-old air that has sat stagnant underground for three centuries. It's the last place on Earth—or in the earth, anyway—that I want to go. I kick at the zombie, but her grip is stronger than her bony fingers look. She manages to yank me away from El Presidente, leaving Liam to wrestle the demon on his own.

"Oh, bloody *heck*," the demon says, going stiff as Liam does his best to muscle it into submission. "I've had just about enough of this *poop*."

El Presidente reaches down and taps its finger once and then twice onto Liam's head. The demon's horn begins to glow red with rage. I see the hair on Liam's head rise toward the sky as the air surrounding us fills with electricity.

"You picked the wrong side of the fight," El Presidente tells Liam.

There's suddenly an immense flash of light. It blinds me for a moment. As my eyes adjust, I search the area for Liam. But I don't see him anywhere. Instead, all that remains is a guinea pig with the same aura he has.

"Oh no," I say out loud. We're totally

fog-waddled, and both El Presidente and I know it.

The demon turns to me as two more zombies burst up out of the ground and grab hold of me. Between the new arrivals and Prudence, I'm pinned in place, unable to move.

"I have to give you credit," El Presidente says to me, stepping closer. "I didn't think you and your friends had it in you to make this interesting. But as it turns out, El Presidente is mildly amused. Mostly annoyed . . . but still amused."

I try to break free of the zombies, but I'm unable to gain enough leverage while lying on my back. I know that I just need to give Bella and Addie a few more minutes to complete the spell. It's the only chance we've got. Maybe I can try and stall by talking to the demon? It's worth a shot.

I've completely forgotten about Screech, though. Before I can put my own plan into action, Madelyn has moved forward with hers. She pilots the drone straight down into El Presidente's head. At first, I think the move will do little more than irritate the demon. But as it turns out, a drone's propellers can get tangled up in a demon's hair the same as they can in a human's.

The demon howls as its hair twists and turns in Screech's propellers, yanking the follicles at the roots. El Presidente flails around, trying to pull itself free. But the more it struggles, the more snarled it gets.

Meanwhile, I am still struggling to free myself from the zombies when I spot Madelyn climbing up onto the rock wall that surrounds the cemetery. She cups her hands around her mouth and shouts out in my direction.

"Bella is almost done! Keep at it and don't die!"

Easier said than done. Not only has my best friend—whom I'm not even sure I can call that anymore—been turned into a pet store rodent, but I'm seconds away from being pulled apart by a trio of surprisingly strong zombies. Oh yeah, and El Presidente has just smashed Screech into a thousand little plastic pieces, thus destroying the distraction that was surely keeping me alive.

"I don't suppose you're still amused?" I ask the demon as it stands over me, snarling.

El Presidente doesn't respond. Instead, it reaches down and rips Prudence Danworth's tombstone from the ground. I can't be sure, but I believe I hear the Prudence zombie sucking at its own teeth, as if it resents its grave marker being desecrated.

El Presidente raises the tombstone above its head—above *my* head—and prepares to bring it down on me. I think about Dad and how I'm never going to get to see him again. My heart sinks, but I try to find peace in the fact that at least I can tell Mom how much Dad and I have missed her.

15

"I'll see you in *heck*," El Presidente says, ready to drop Prudence's tombstone onto my head.

Out of the corner of my eye, I see a critter scurrying toward the demon. At first, I assume it's a rat given the setting. But then I realize it's a guinea pig.

The demon is so filled with wrath that it doesn't notice that guinea pig-Liam is now standing below. He opens his tiny, adorable guinea pig jaws and then drives his incisors into the demon's foot.

Black blood spurts out of the wounds as the demon squeals and stumbles backward. El Presidente's grip on the tombstone falters. The tombstone drops from its grasp and smashes onto its own head. This appears to stun El Presidente as it stumbles side to side.

Prudence seems appalled by her grave

marker's destruction. She loosens her grip long enough for me to wriggle free from both her and her zombie cohorts.

I scramble back to my feet as the demon hops around on one leg, trying to stomp down on Liam. While El Presidente is distracted, I drive my shoulder into its back, knocking it into one of the many open graves that now surround us. El Presidente lands some six feet below with a loud *thump*.

"That's it!" El Presidente screams from inside the empty grave. "I was going to do this apocalypse the nice way, but now you've left me with no *frogging* choice!"

A bolt of bluish lightning spits down from the sky and strikes inside the open grave where the demon is tucked away. The sky turns black—so black that it appears to disappear completely.

There is a loud shriek from somewhere in the distance. The noise is coming from no discernible direction because it seems to be coming from everywhere. It's as if the planet itself is screaming.

"We're too late," I say, my stomach plummeting.

I close my eyes, not wanting to see the world unravel in front of me. I think about the good times I've had throughout my rather short life. My days spent with family, especially my dad, but also my mom, with whom I had such a brief time. And then, of course, there are my friends, whom I love. Liam, Madelyn, Boo-en. I'm so upset that I'll never see any of them again—that the world itself will never see any of them again.

I wait for it to all go away, but it doesn't. I honestly thought the end of times would sound a lot different. There are no explosions, horrific screams, or even any fizzling squelchy sounds. (Part of me pictured the planet flitting around the universe as it leaked life like a balloon losing its precious air.)

I open my eyes. Through the trees that hang over the cemetery, I can see stars twinkling in their brilliant existence.

I turn my head and take in the scene. Liam in his human form is sitting on the ground.

He is scratching at his neck with his back leg, though, so I guess a part of his rodent form is still lingering.

I step up to the hole in the ground where El Presidente had fallen into. It's empty.

I turn around and look over the cemetery. There are still zombies everywhere, but they look confused. I swear Prudence even shrugs her reanimated shoulders. She looks bored.

I close my eyes once again. What happened? Did we do it?

When I open my eyes a second time, the zombies are gone. It's not even as if they disappeared out of thin air. It's more like they never came to life at all.

The ground and all the graves are completely covered with soil again. Even Prudence's grave maker is back in one piece, sticking upright out of her final (hopefully) resting place. Screech is perched on top of the tombstone, also whole again.

In the distance, Addie and Bella peek up and over the wall that surrounds the cemetery. They look hopeful.

"Did it work?" Addie asks.

I spin around and help a confused Liam to his feet. "I think it did!" I shout in response. "Does anyone see any adults around? Are they unfrozen?"

Madelyn's voice calls out from the other side of the cemetery. "Eyes on a few over here! They look totally back to normal. Baffled, but back to normal!"

I pull Liam to me and hug him before he can pull away. "You saved my life!"

"Duh," he says, pulling back from my hug, but not to avoid it. I was just squeezing him so hard that he couldn't breathe. "You're my best friend."

My eyes light up. "Are we still?"

Liam reaches out and punches me in my shoulder, nearly knocking me off my feet. That one will leave a bruise.

"Of course we're still best friends. Stop being such a human."

"It's just, you were so mad at me. You had every right to be, and I was totally wrong about how I handled the situation at the Mexican restaurant. I'll do a better job going forward. I'm going to go out of my way to—"

"Damon!" Liam shouts, causing me to skid out of my uncontrolled rambling. "I spoke my piece about it. I never said I was going to be mad at you forever. In fact, I wasn't even mad, per se. I was more . . . hurt. But still, seeing how much that you care that I cared, that means a lot. It tells me that I'm not just any other demon to you."

"Because you're not," I assure him. "You're . . ."

Liam rolls his eyes. "Don't say it!"

". . . my demon!"

"Ugh," Liam exclaims, walking away from me. "Gag me with a pitchfork."

"You can think it's cheesy, but it's true!"

"Yay for me," Liam says sarcastically.

We exit the cemetery and meet up with Madelyn, who is controlling Screech so that the drone is following us overhead. Together, we all head back to the opposite side of the Friends Burial Ground where we find Addie and Bella.

"So, is like, everything fixed?" Bella asks, using her foot to erase the witchcraft symbols drawn on the sidewalk.

I nod. "I think so. We'll have to all check in with our families and make sure there aren't any lasting effects from the freeze on them, but I think that Clip Hex of yours did the trick. Whoever says five seconds can't make a difference, I'll refer them back to the time that five seconds saved the world!"

Addie shuffles back and forth. She's clearly uncomfortable now that her adrenaline has plummeted to a somewhat normal level.

"So, I mean, I guess now would be the time for me to apologize to everyone for almost bringing about the complete end of everything, right?"

I smile. It's hard not to. "It's not only your fault, Addie. I should have made it clear just how dangerous it was for you to be messing around with demons. If I hadn't been so worried about keeping our demon hunting under wraps, we probably never would have been in this situation in the first place."

I pause. No one refutes me. "Also, I was distracted. Same as you. Liam and I were not speaking, and it was taking me off my game, big time."

"I can relate to that," she says, miming herself taking a shot in a basketball game. There's no telling if she made the basket in her imagination or not, but if it was taken in reality, I have no doubt that she would have.

"This is all super heartfelt and gooey in that way only a couple of humans can turn a close-call apocalypse into, but can we all just go home now?" Liam asks. "Not only do I have to reckon with the fact that I was turned into a guinea pig, but I also still have a ton of biology homework to do."

"I almost forgot about mine," I say, realizing that I still have a page sitting on my desk with nothing but my name attached to it.

We all turn around in unison, expecting to see Bella's family minivan waiting to take us back home. Only, it's not there.

By editing out those five seconds from our timeline, we also edited out our ride as the minivan is, no doubt, still safely parked in Bella's garage.

"Well," I say, resigning to the fact that we have no other choice, "I guess we're all walking home."

ABOUT THE AUTHOR

When not writing in his spiral notebooks, Jason M. Burns can be found outside getting his tattoo-covered arms dirty where he spends the warmer months hybridizing daylilies and tending to his koi pond. Type A even when typing, he has written and created a number of critically-acclaimed and commercially successful comic book series and graphic novels, including *Magical Pet Vet* and *Jericho: Season 3*, which appeared on the *New York Times* Best Sellers list. He has spearheaded book lines for *Sesame Street* and the DreamWorks Animation stable of titles and most recently served as Chief Creative Officer for Neymar Jr. Comics, the publishing company of international soccer star Neymar Jr. There his writing was translated across six languages and reached over forty million people worldwide. In addition to comic books, Burns also works in Hollywood where he has a number of television and film projects in development. He is also co-host of the popular podcast series *What About*, which he produces alongside actor Danny Nucci (*Titanic*, *The Fosters*).

Burns lives in Massachusetts with his wife, two children, and a trio of rescue dogs with unnecessarily silly names, Bark W. Grizwold, Maisy Gray, and Bad Bad Leroy Brown.